A TEMPLAR BOOK

Produced by The Templar Company plc,
Pippbrook Mill, London Road, Dorking, Surrey RH4 1JE, Great Britain.

This edition produced for Parragon Books,
Unit 13-17, Avonbridge Trading Estate, Atlantic Road, Avonmouth, Bristol BS11 9QD

This book contains material first published as
*The Disappointed Sprites* in Enid Blyton's Teacher's Treasury 1926.

Illustrated by Isobel Bushell

Printed and bound in Italy

ISBN 1-85813-633-4

*Enid Blyton's*

POCKET LIBRARY

# THE DISAPPOINTED SPRITES

## Illustrated by Isobel Bushell

·PARRAGON·

Once upon a time the little water-sprites were very sad. They sat swinging in the rushes that grew by the side of the lake, and talked about their trouble.

"I don't think it's fair!" said Willow. "Why shouldn't we be allowed to dance in the fairy-ring too! I do think that the fairies are mean!"

"Is it *really* true that they said we weren't to dance with them any more?" asked Trickle.

"Yes, didn't you know?" said
Splashabout. "They sent us a letter
this morning. Read it, Willow."

Willow took a letter from her
pocket and spread it out. "This is
what they say," she began. "Dear
Water-Sprites, please do not
come and dance in our
fairy-ring any more.
You spoil our dances.
With love from
the Fairies."

"Well! How very horrid of them!" cried Trickle. "Why don't they want us any more? We behave quite nicely!"

"Let's go and ask them!" said Splashabout. "And if we think their reason is fair, we won't make a fuss. But if it isn't, we'll go and complain to the Queen."

So the three little sprites set off over the grass to Pixie-town among the toadstools. Here were fairies and elves, pixies and brownies.

They all stared at the three sprites as they came running up, and wondered what was the matter.

"What do you want?" they cried. "Have you lost something?"

"No," answered Willow, "but we want to know why we aren't allowed to come and dance with you any more. What have we done to upset you?"

"Nothing," said a fairy. "It isn't really your fault."

"Well, whose fault is it, then?" asked Splashabout impatiently. "We think it's very mean of you."

The pixies and fairies looked at each other. Nobody wanted to explain. At last a brownie broke the silence.

"It's like this," he said. "You're always so *wet*, and when we dance with you we spoil our clothes."

"And you make all the seats wet too, with your damp frocks," said an elf.

"And I've got a dreadful cold through putting on one of your wet shawls by mistake. A-tishoo! A-tishoo!" said a pixie, and blew his nose loudly.

The sprites stared sadly at the fairies.

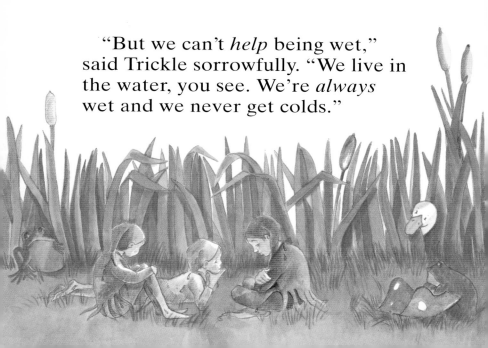

"But we can't *help* being wet," said Trickle sorrowfully. "We live in the water, you see. We're *always* wet and we never get colds."

"That's because you're used to it," said a fairy. "We aren't, and we feel as if we're dancing with frogs when we dance with you.

"We're awfully sorry about it, but you do spoil all our dances."

The three water-sprites looked at each other, and decided to be brave about it.

"We're sorry," said Willow. "We quite understand."

"But it's dreadfully disappointing, because we do so like dancing," said Trickle, nearly crying.

"And there's no place on the water where we can dance," said Splashabout.

They said goodbye, and went sadly back to the lake. They told all the water-sprites what they had heard, and everyone was very upset.

"That's the end of all our dancing," said Ripple. "And it's a great pity, for we are the lightest and daintiest of all fairy folk."

"Well, we must just make the best of it," said Willow. "We'll go and watch next time the fairies have a dance, but we won't go near enough to wet them."

So next time the elves and fairies held a dance in the fairy-ring, the sprites crept up to watch them. They heard the music played by the grasshoppers and bees, and longed to join in the dance, but they had made up their minds to be good – and so they were.

Carefully they hid themselves in the long grass around the fairy-ring and peeped out from behind the wild flowers to watch quietly.

Now, it happened that the Fairy Queen decided to go to the dance that night. She floated down, pale and beautiful in the moonlight, and took her place on the little silver throne that always stood waiting for her.

The fairies were delighted to see her, and made a great fuss of her, for she was very good to them.

"Go on with your dancing," she said. "I'd love to watch you."

So they all danced and tripped,

and pranced and skipped, as merry as could be, till suddenly the Queen wondered where the water-sprites were. They had never missed a dance before, and she couldn't think why they weren't there. She peeped all round the dancers, but not one sprite could she see.

And then she suddenly spied them peeping and peering behind the buttercups and daisies outside the fairy-ring! She *was* astonished!

She clapped her hands and ordered the dance to stop for a minute. The music stopped and everyone turned to hear what Her Majesty had to say.

"Why do the water-sprites peep and hide, instead of dancing?" she asked. "Have they been naughty?"

"Oh no, Your Majesty!" answered a pixie. "They're not at all naughty. But we asked them not to come to our dances any more."

"Why did you do that?" asked the Queen in astonishment.

"Because they are always so dreadfully wet!" answered the pixie. "They ruin our clothes and make us catch terrible colds."

"But haven't they anywhere to dance now?" asked the Queen.

"No, nowhere," said the pixie, sadly. "They can't dance on the lake, you see, and we can't have them in our dancing-rings any more."

"Dear, dear!" said the Queen. "Whatever can we do! Were the water-sprites nice about it, or were they angry?"

"They were ever so nice," said all the fairies at once.

"They promised not to come!" said a brownie.

"And they said they were sorry and quite understood!" called an elf.

The Queen was pleased. She liked to hear of people taking a

disappointment cheerfully. She waved her hand.

"Go on with your dancing," she said, looking thoughtful.

The bees and grasshoppers began playing again, and the fairies took their partners and went merrily on with their dance.

They didn't see the Queen slip away through the grass. She went very quietly, her crown gleaming like dewdrops in the bright moonlight.

She went to the lake. It lay very peaceful and still. All the sprites who usually played there were away watching the dance.

Big white and yellow water-lilies lay on the water. The Queen called to them.

"Water-lilies," she cried, "where are your leaves?"

"Down in the water!" answered the water-lilies in voices like a hundred singing ripples.

"Listen!" said the Queen. "Raise them to the top of the lake, and let them spread themselves smooth and flat on the water." The lilies all raised their leaves and did as they were told. Gradually the lake became spread with big flat leaves, shining in the moonlight.

"Thank you," said the Queen. "You look beautiful now, water-lilies. Will you let the little water-sprites dance on your leaves when the lake is calm?"

"Yes! Yes!" said the water-lilies softly. "We love the water-sprites; they look after our buds for us!"

Then the Queen called the green frogs to her, and told each to fetch his instrument and climb on to the water-lily leaves and play a merry tune.

"Yes, Your Majesty!" they cried, and clambered quickly up. Then they struck up such a loud merry tune that all the fairies and sprites away by the dancing-ring listened in astonishment. Then they all ran helter-skelter to the lake to see what the music could be.

There they found the Queen, sitting on a water-lily, with the frogs playing their instruments as merrily as could be.

"Look! Look!" cried the fairies. "The water-lilies have brought their leaves to the surface!"

"What fun! What fun!" cried the water-sprites, jumping on to the leaves. "Oh, Your Majesty, we could dance on these! May we?"

"Yes, you may!" answered the Queen smiling. "And now, whenever the fairies hold a dance in the fairy-ring, *you* may hold a dance on the lily leaves, for the frogs will play for you until dawn!"

"Oh, thank you, thank you!"
cried the sprites in great delight.
They each took a partner and
were soon gaily dancing
on the smooth lily
leaves, whilst the
fairies looked
on in wonder.

When dawn came, nothing was to be seen of the Queen or the fairies. The water-sprites were gone, and so were the frogs and their instruments. But calm and steady the water-lily leaves floated on the water, waiting for the time when little feet should dance on them once again.

Look at them, next time you pass by a lake. The biggest leaf you see is the one that the Queen sits on. Don't you think it was a splendid idea of hers?